THE ADVENTURES OF GRANDMASAURUS

Written by
Caroline Fernandez

Illustrated by
Shannon O'Toole

COMMON DEER PRESS

Published by Common Deer Press Incorporated.

Copyright © 2020 Caroline Fernandez and Shannon O'Toole

All rights reserved under International and Pan-American Copyright Conventions. No part of this book may be reproduced in any form or by any electronic or mechanical means, including information storage and retrieval systems, without permission in writing from the publisher, except by a reviewer, who may quote brief passages in a review.

Published in 2020 by Common Deer Press 3203-1 Scott St. Toronto, ON M5V 1A1
This book is a work of fiction. Names, characters, places, and incidents are either the product of the author's imagination or are used fictitiously.

Cover Image and Illustrations: © Shannon O'Toole
Book Design: David Moratto

Library of Congress Cataloging-in-Publication Data First edition.
The Adventures of Grandmasaurus / Caroline Fernandez and Shannon O'Toole
ISBN: 978-1-988761-45-9 (softcover) ISBN: 978-1-988761-46-6 (hardcover)

Printed in Canada

Common Deer Press www.commondeerpress.com

But a silver sparkle of museum dust soared up Grandma's nose.
Dust + sneezing = Grandma's funny business.

Ah . . . Ah . . . CHOO!
Grandma disappeared. Poof!

"Uh-oh," I whispered.
"Not again!" Moonie cried. "Where is she?"

We looked high and low.
"No. No. No." I quietly moaned.

Then we spotted her.

"What kind of dinosaur IS she?!" Moonie asked.

I looked at our museum study pages. "E-o-rap-tor."
"Small. Fast. Light." Moonie read over my shoulder.

Grandma zoomed off.
"Grandma, you can't RUN in a museum!"

And then Grandma Eoraptor sneezed
. . . *Ah . . . Ah . . . CHOO!*

"What now?!" I wondered.
"There!" Moonie gasped.
Moonie grabbed the study pages from my hands. "Zu-ni-cera-tops." she said.
"Big as a cow. Horns. Slow."
Grandma Zuniceratops stood there like a wall.

"Grandma, you can't block the exhibits," I said. "It's against the rules! Grandma, move over . . . please!"
Then she let out another great, big,
Ah . . . Ah . . . CHOO!

"She's over there!" Moonie pointed. "An-k-lya-saur-us. Walks slowly. Lives in a herd . . ."

"And has body armor" I said. Grandma Anklyasaurus walked up to a plant and started nibbling on the leaves.

I heard Grandma going down
a flight of stairs.

Bump. Bump. Bump. Bump.

We followed.
When I saw the cafeteria sign, I knew . . .

"No butting in line!" I said.
"You have to wait your turn like everybody else."

Ah . . . Ah . . . CHOO!
Poof! She was gone. Again.

"Good thing she hasn't turned into a T-rex," Moonie said.
"She'd be a handful."
"Good thing?! There's no good thing here!" I exclaimed.
"Grandma keeps running off doing funny business. On a field trip!
And if she doesn't stop, we'll miss the school bus."

Then, we heard a moo. A roar. A moo-roar. It was coming from the lobby.

"Wowzers, she's as big as a building!" Moonie proclaimed.
"Brach-i-o-saur-us. Herbivore. Long neck." I whispered.

Grandma Brachiosaurus moo-roared again.
"STOP," I said. "Where's your indoor voice?!
You can't yell in a museum!"

Ah . . . Ah . . . CHOO!

"No. Hard no! That's it!" I said. "You need a time-out, Grandma! You aren't allowed to fly in a museum. No. No. No."

"And," Moonie added, "pterodactyls aren't even dinosaurs. They're flying reptiles. Nice try, Grandma!"

"Where'd she go?!"
I asked Moonie.
We searched all the museum floors. We checked the washrooms. We looked in the gift shop.
"Where could she be?!"
I exclaimed.

"Let's go to the lost children's area." Moonie suggested.
"Why? We aren't lost. Grandma's lost. WE LOST GRANDMA!"

"Exactly . . . and where would anyone go when they are lost at the museum? The lost children's area! Look . . . there she is!" Moonie yelled.
"Tro-o-don." I said.
"The smartest dinosaur of them all!"
I checked our study pages. "Half the size of a grown-up human. Sharp teeth. Toe claws."

"Grandmasaurus we found you!"

AH... AH...

With the last sneeze Grandma turned back into regular Grandma.
Just in time to get on the school bus.

"Can I come on your next field trip?" Grandma asked. "No funny business."